FRENCH
FOR BEGINNERS

Illustrated by John Shackell
Designed by Roger Priddy

Language consultant: Françoise Holmes

CONTENTS

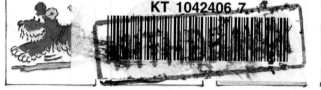

Handlettering by Jack Potter

About this book

Going abroad is much more fun if you can speak a little of the language. This book shows you that learning another language is a lot easier than you might think. It teaches you the French you will find useful in everyday situations.

You can find out how to . . .

talk about yourself,

and your home,

count and tell the time,

say what you like,

find your way around

and ask for what you want in shops.

How you learn

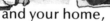

Picture strips like this show you what to say in each situation. Read the speech bubbles and see how much you can understand by yourself, then look up any words you do not know. Words and phrases are repeated again and again, to help you remember them.

The book starts with really easy things to say and gets more difficult towards the end.

New words

All the new words you come across are listed on each double page, so you can look them up as you go along. If you forget any words you can look them up in the glossary on pages 46-48. *If you see an asterisk by a word, it means that there is a note about it at the bottom of the page.

Grammar

Boxes like this around words show where new grammar is explained. You will find French easier if you learn some of its grammar, or rules, but don't worry if you don't understand it all straightaway. You can look up any of the grammar used in the book on pages 42-43.

Internet links*

At the top of each double page you will find descriptions of useful websites for learning French. For links to these sites, go to **www.usborne-quicklinks.com** and enter the keywords **french for beginners**.

Puzzles

Throughout this book there are puzzles and quizzes to solve (see answers on pages 44-45). You can also find picture puzzles to print out on the Usborne Quicklinks Website at **www.usborne-quicklinks.com**

Practising your French

Write all the new words you learn in a notebook and try to learn a few every day. Keep going over them and you will soon remember them.

Ask a friend to keep testing you on your French. Even better, ask someone to learn French with you so that you can practise on each other.

Je voudrais...

Try to go to France for your holidays, and speak as much French as you can. Don't be afraid of making mistakes. No one will mind.

* For more information on using the Internet, see inside the front cover.

Saying hello

Here you can find out the different French greetings for different times of the day.

salut — hi, hello, bye
bonjour — hello, good morning
au revoir — goodbye
bonsoir — good evening
bonne nuit — goodnight
à bientôt — see you soon

When you greet someone in French, it is polite to add one of these words: **monsieur** (Sir, Mr.), **madame** (Madam, Mrs.) or **mademoiselle** (Miss).

Saying hello

This is how you say "hello" to your friends.

This is how you greet someone you don't know well.

This is how you say "good evening" to someone.

Saying goodbye

Salut can mean "bye" as well as "hello" or "hi".

Au revoir means "goodbye" and **à bientôt** means "see you soon".

Saying goodnight

You only say **bonne nuit** last thing at night.

How are you?

This is how you ask someone how they are.

The person on the right is saying: "I'm fine, thank you"...

...but this person is saying that he is not very well.

Ça va? (How are you?)

This list gives you the French words you need to talk about how people are.

ça va?	how are you?
ça va bien	I'm fine
merci	thank you
très bien	very well
bien	well
assez bien	quite well
pas très bien	not very well

Which two of the people on the right are saying **ça va bien**?*

*Remember, answers to puzzles are on pages 44-45.

5

What is your name?

Here you can find out how to ask someone their name and tell them yours, and how to introduce your friends. Read the picture strip and see how much you can understand. Then try doing the puzzles on the page opposite.

New words

je	I
tu	you
il	he
elle	she
ils	they (male)
elles	they (female)
comment tu t'appelles?	what are you called?
comment il/elle s'appelle?	what is he /she called?
comment ils s'appellent?	what are they called?
je m'appelle	I am called
il s'appelle	he is called
elle s'appelle	she is called
ils/elles s'appellent	they are called
qui c'est?	who is that?
c'est	that is
mon ami	my friend (male)
mon amie	my friend (female)
et toi?	and you?
oui	yes
non	no

Ils and elles

There are two words for "they" in French: **ils** and **elles**. When you are talking about boys or men, you say **ils** and when you are talking about girls or women, you say **elles**.

If you are talking about boys and girls together, you say **ils**.

Bonjour, Comment tu t'appelles?

Max, et toi?

Je m'appelle Monique.

Introducing friends

C'est mon ami. Il s'appelle Pierre.

Qui c'est?

C'est mon amie. Elle s'appelle Marie.

Comment ils s'appellent?

Ils s'appellent Paul et Jean.

What are they called?

Can you answer these questions in French?

Comment elle s'appelle, mon amie?

Comment tu t'appelles ?

Comment il s'appelle?

Comment ils s'appellent?

Who is who?

Can you answer the questions below the picture?

Salut, ça va ?

Ça va bien, merci.

Au revoir, Nicolas.

C'est Anne?

Oui, c'est Anne.

Au revoir.

C'est Jean.

Qui c'est ?

Non, je m'appelle Michel.

Tu t'appelles Max ?

Comment tu t'appelles ?

Pascale, et toi?

Who is talking to Jean?   Who is called Michel?   Who is called Anne?
Who is talking to Pascale?   Who is talking to him?   Who is going home?

Can you remember?

How would you ask someone their name?
How would you tell them your name?

You have a friend called Pascale. How would you introduce her to someone?
How would you tell someone your friend is called Daniel?

7

Finding out what things are called.

Everything on this picture has its name on it. See if you can learn the names for everything, then try the memory test at the bottom of the opposite page. You can find out what **le**, **la** and **l'** mean at the bottom of the page.

le soleil

la cheminée

le toit

l'oiseau

le nid

Bonjour!

l'arbre

la fenêtre

la fleur

la maison

la porte

le garage

Ça, c'est ma maison.

la barrière

le chien

le chat

la voiture

Le and la words

All French nouns are either masculine or feminine. The word you use for "the" shows what gender the noun is. The word for "the" is **le** before masculine (m) nouns, **la** before feminine (f) ones and **l'** before those which start with a vowel. It is best to learn which word to use with each noun. "A" or "an" is **un** before **le** words and **une** before **la** words.

le soleil	sun	**le nid**	nest	**la fenêtre**	window
l'arbre(m)	tree	**l'oiseau(m)**	bird	**la porte**	door
le toit	roof	**le garage**	garage	**la fleur**	flower
le chat	cat	**la maison**	house	**la voiture**	car
le chien	dog	**la cheminée**	chimney	**la barrière**	fence

Asking what things are called

Don't worry if you don't know what something is called in French. To find out what it is, just ask someone **qu'est-ce que c'est?** Look at the list of useful phrases below, then read the picture strip to see how to use them.

qu'est-ce que c'est?	what is that?
c'est . . .	that is . . .
aussi	also
en français	in French
en anglais	in English

Can you remember?

Cover up the opposite page and see if you can name all of these things in French. Don't forget to say whether they are **le** or **la** words.

9

Where do you come from?

Here you can find out how to ask people where they come from. You can also find out how to ask if they speak French.

New words

tu viens d'où?	where do you come from?
je viens de* . .	I come from . .
tu habites où?	where do you live?
j'habite . .	I live in . .
tu parles . . **?**	do you speak . . ?
je parle . .	I speak . .
un petit peu	a little
français	French
anglais	English
allemand	German
voici	this is
nous	we
vous	you (plural)

Countries

l'Afrique(f)	Africa
l'Allemagne(f)	Germany
l'Angleterre(f)	England
la France	France
l'Inde(f)	India
l'Écosse(f)	Scotland
l'Autriche(f)	Austria
l'Espagne	Spain
la Hongrie	Hungary

Where do you come from?

Do you speak French?

*__De__ means "from". Before a word beginning with a vowel, it changes to **d'**: **je viens d'Angleterre** (I come from England).

Who comes from where?

These are the contestants for an international dancing competition. They have come from all over the world. The compère does not speak any French and does not understand where anyone comes from. Read about the contestants then see if you can tell him what he wants to know. His questions are beneath the picture.

Angus vient d'Ecosse.

Voici Marie et Pierre. Ils viennent de France.

Hari et Indira viennent d'Inde.

Yuri vient de Hongrie. Il habite Budapest.

Franz vient d'Autriche.

Where do they all come from?

Voici Lolita. Elle vient d'Espagne.

Where does Franz come from?
What are the French contestants called?
Is Lolita Italian or Spanish?

Is there a Scottish contestant?
Where do Marie and Pierre come from?
Who lives in Budapest? Where is Budapest?

Verbs (action words)	**parler**	to speak	**venir**	to come

French verbs change according to who is doing the action. Verbs ending in **er** follow the same pattern and have the same endings as **parler**. You will have to learn **venir** by itself.*	**je parle**
	tu parles
	il/elle parle
	nous parlons
	vous parlez
	ils/elles
	   parlent
		I speak
		you speak
		he/she speaks
		we speak
		you speak
		
		they speak
			je viens
			tu viens
			il/elle vient
			nous venons
			vous venez
			ils/elles
			   viennent
				I come
				you come
				he/she comes
				we come
				you come
				
				they come

Can you remember?

How would you ask someone where they come from?

Can you say where you come from?
How do you say that you speak French?
How would you ask someone if they can?

*You can find out more about verbs on page 43.

More about you

Here you can find out how to count up to 20, say how old you are and say how many brothers and sisters you have.

To say how old you are in French, you say how many years you have. So if you are ten, you say **J'ai dix ans** (I have ten years).

New words

quel âge as tu?	how old are you?
j'ai cinq ans	I am five years old
as-tu..?	have you . . ?
j'ai	I have
je n'ai pas de	I have no
des	some, any
le frère	brother
la soeur	sister
presque	almost
ni	nor
mais	but

Plural words

Most French nouns add an "s" in the plural (when you are talking about more than one person or thing), but you don't pronounce it. There are some exceptions which you can see in the glossary. The word for "the" is **les** before all plural nouns.

Numbers*

1	un/une	11	onze
2	deux	12	douze
3	trois	13	treize
4	quatre	14	quatorze
5	cinq	15	quinze
6	six	16	seize
7	sept	17	dix-sept
8	huit	18	dix-huit
9	neuf	19	dix-neuf
10	dix	20	vingt

How old are you?

Quel âge as-tu ?

J'ai douze ans, et toi ?

J'ai onze ans.

Have you any brothers and sisters?

Tu as des frères et des soeurs ?

Oui, j'ai un frère et une soeur.

Quel âge ont-ils ?

Mon frère a dix ans et ma soeur a neuf ans.

Je n'ai pas de frères ni de soeurs.

*You will find a complete list of numbers on page 40.

How old are they?

Read what these children are saying, then see if you can say how old they all are.

Guy a douze ans.

Nous avons quinze ans.

Odile a onze ans.

Michel a presque quatorze ans.

J'ai cinq ans. Il a neuf ans.

Michel   Diane et Sylvie   Guy   Odile   Luc   Colette

How many brothers and sisters?

Below you can read how many brothers and sisters the children have. Can you work out who has which brothers and sisters?

Diane et Sylvie ont un frère et deux soeurs.

Odile a trois soeurs et deux frères.

Michel a cinq soeurs, mais pas de frères.

Luc a un frère, mais pas de soeurs.

Guy n'a pas de frères ni de soeurs, mais il a un chien.

Useful verbs

avoir	to have
j'ai	I have
tu as	you have
il/elle a	he/she/it has
nous avons	we have
vous avez	you have
ils/elles ont	they have

être*	to be
je suis	I am
tu es	you are
il/elle est	he/she/it is
nous sommes	we are
vous êtes	you are
ils/elles sont	they are

*Être is used on the next page, so it may help you to learn it now.

Talking about your family

On these two pages you will learn lots of words which will help you to talk about your family. You will also find out how to say "my" and "your" and describe people.

> Voici ma famille.

mon chien

mon grand-père

mon père

ma soeur

mon oncle

mon chat

ma grand-mère

ma mère

mon frère

ma tante

Who's who?

> C'est ton frère ?

> Oui, c'est mon frère.

> Et ça, c'est ta soeur?

> Oui, elle s'appelle Nathalie.

> Ce sont tes parents ?

> Non! Ce sont mes grands-parents!

New words

la famille	family	**la tante**	aunt	**mince**	thin
le grand-père	grandfather	**les grands-parents**	grandparents	**vieux***	old
la grand-mère	grandmother	**les parents**	parents	**jeune**	young
le père	father	**grand/e**	tall	**blond/e**	blonde
la mère	mother	**petit/e**	small	**brun/e**	dark-haired
l'oncle(m)	uncle	**gros/se**	fat	**affectueux/se**	friendly

How to say "my" and "your"

The word you use for "my" or "your" depends on whether you are talking about a **le**, **la** or plural word.*

	my	your
le words	**mon**	**ton**
la words	**ma**	**ta**
plurals	**mes**	**tes**

*You use **mon** or **ton** before words beginning with a vowel. You can find out more about this on pages 42-43.

Describing your family

> Mon père est grand et ma mère est petite.

> Ma mère est grande et mon père est petit.

> Mon oncle est gros et ma tante est mince.

> Mon grand-père est très vieux.* Je suis jeune.

> Ma soeur est blonde. Mon frère est brun.

> Mon chien est affectueux.

Describing words

French adjectives change their endings depending on whether they are describing a **le** or **la** word. In the word list the masculine form is shown, along with the letters you add to make it feminine. The **"x"** on the end of **affectueux** changes to **"se".***

Can you describe each of these people in French, starting **Il est . .** or **Elle est . . ?**

*You can find out more about adjectives on pages 42-43. The feminine of **vieux** is **vieille**.

Your home

Here you can find out how to say what sort of home you live in and whereabouts it is. You can also learn what all the rooms are called.

New words

ou	or
la maison	house
l'appartement(m)	flat
le château	castle
en ville	in the town
à la campagne	in the country
au bord de la mer	by the sea
papa	Dad
maman	Mum
pépé	Grandad
mémé	Granny
le fantôme	ghost
où êtes-vous?	where are you?
la salle de bains	bathroom
la salle à manger	dining room
la chambre	bedroom
le salon	living room
la cuisine	kitchen
le vestibule	hall
en haut	upstairs

Where do you live?

Tu habites une maison ou un appartement?

J'habite une maison.

J'habite un appartement.

J'habite un château.

Town or country?

J'habite en ville.

J'habite à la campagne.

J'habite au bord de la mer.

Where is everyone?

Papa comes home and wants to know where everyone is. Look at the pictures and see if you can tell him where everyone is, e.g. **Mémé est** **dans le salon**. Then see if you can answer the questions below the little pictures.

Maman   Papa   Pépé

Mémé   Pierre   Isabelle

Simon   le fantôme

Je suis dans la salle de bains

Je suis en haut !

Je suis dans la chambre d'Isabelle.

Je suis dans le salon.

Je suis dans la chambre.

Où êtes-vous ?

Je suis dans la salle à manger.

Je suis dans la cuisine

Qui est dans la salle à manger?
Qui est dans la cuisine?
Qui est dans la salle de bains?
Qui est dans la chambre?

Où est mémé?
Où est le fantôme?
Où est le chien?
Où est Pierre?
Où est papa? (Look at the word list)

Can you remember?

How do you ask someone where they live?
How do you ask whether they live in a house or a flat?

Can you remember how to say "in the country"?
Can you remember how to say "in the town"?

How would you tell someone you were upstairs?
How would you tell them you were in the kitchen?

Looking for things

Here you can find out how to ask someone what they are looking for and tell them where things are. You can also learn lots of words for things around the house.

New words

chercher	to look for
quelque chose	something
le hamster	hamster
trouver	to find
le	him/it
sur	on
sous	under
derrière	behind
devant	in front of
entre	between
à côté de	next to
le placard	cupboard
l'armoire(f)	wardrobe
le fauteuil	armchair
le rideau	curtain
la plante	plant
le rayon	shelf
la table	table
le tapis	carpet
le canapé	sofa
la télévision	television
le téléphone	telephone
le vase	vase
le voilà!	there it is!

Il or elle?

There isn't a special word for "it" in French. You use **il** or **elle** ("he" or "she") depending on whether the word you are replacing is masculine or feminine. You use **il** to replace masculine words and **elle** to replace feminine ones.

Où est **le** hamster?
Il est sur la table.

Où est **la** tortue?
Elle est sur la table.

The missing hamster

Tu cherches quelque chose?

Je cherche mon hamster. Je ne le trouve pas!

Il n'est pas sur l'armoire.

Il n'est pas sous le canapé.

Il est derrière le rideau?

Non.

Le voilà! Entre les plantes!

18

In, on or under?

Try to learn these words by heart. **A côté de** changes to **à côte du** when you put it before a **le** word, e.g. **à côté du fauteuil** (next to the armchair.)

dans   derrière   devant   à côté de   sous   sur

Where are they hiding?

Monsieur Hulot's six pets are hiding somewhere in the room, but he cannot find them. Can you tell him where they are in French, using the words above?

le hamster

le petit chat

le petit chien

la perruche

le serpent

la tortue

le rayon

le vase

le placard

la télévision

le téléphone

le tapis

la table

le fauteuil

le canapé

What do you like eating?

Here you can find out how to say what you like and don't like.

New words

aimer	to like
tu aimes?	do you like?
j'aime	I like
je n'aime pas*	I don't like
qu'est-ce que . .	what . . ?
adorer	to like a lot
pas du tout	not at all
alors	then
beaucoup	very much
le plus	the most
préférer	to prefer
surtout	best of all
la salade	salad
le poisson	fish
les pommes frites	chips
le gâteau	cake
la saucisse	sausage
le bifteck	steak
les spaghetti (m pl)	spaghetti
manger	to eat
la pizza	pizza
le hamburger	hamburger
le riz	rice
le pain	bread
le fromage	cheese
moi aussi	me too

What do you like?

Tu aimes la salade?

Tu aimes le poisson?

Non, je n'aime pas la salade.

Non, pas du tout

Qu'est-ce que tu aimes, alors?

Et j'adore les gâteaux!

J'aime les pommes frites.

What do you like best?

Qu'est-ce que tu aimes le plus?

J'aime beaucoup les saucisses.

. . . Mais je préfère le bifteck.

.. Et j'aime surtout les spaghetti!

20   *You can read more about negatives on pages 42-43.

What are they eating?

Qu'est-ce que tu manges?

Je mange une pizza.

Elle mange des frites.

Il mange du pain et du fromage.

Nous mangeons des hamburgers.

Vous mangez du riz.

Ils mangent des bananes.

Who likes what?

Who likes cheese? Who doesn't like ham? Who prefers grapes to bananas?

Can you say in French which things you like and which you don't like?

Moi aussi, mais je n'aime pas le jambon

Jean

J'aime les bananes.

Simon

Je préfère le raisin.

Pépé

J'aime surtout la tarte aux fruits

J'aime le fromage.

Boris

Isabelle

le jambon   le beurre   la quiche

le pain

la salade   les tomates   le fromage

les bananes   le raisin   une tarte aux fruits   le jus d'orange

Du, de la, de l' and des

These mean "some" and are often used when there is nothing in English, e.g. **il mange du pain** (he is eating bread). You use **du** before **le** words, **de la** before **la** words, **de l'** before words beginning with a vowel and **des** before plural words.

Table talk

Here you can learn all sorts of useful things to say if you are having a meal with French friends or eating out in a French restaurant.

New words

à table s'il te plaît	come to the table please
j'ai faim	I'm hungry
moi aussi	me too
sers-toi	help yourself
servez-vous	help yourselves
bon appétit	enjoy your meal
tu peux me passer . .	can you pass me . . .
l'eau	water
le pain	bread
le verre	glass
voulez-vous* . . ?	would you like
encore de . .	some more . .
la viande	meat
oui, s'il te plaît	yes please
non, merci	no, thank you
j'ai assez mangé	I've had enough
c'est bon?	is it good?
c'est délicieux	it's delicious

Dinner is ready

Please will you pass me . . .

*Vous is a polite way of saying "you". You can find out more about it on page 30.

Would you like some more?

> Voulez-vous encore de la viande ?

> Oui, merci.

> Voulez-vous encore des frites ?

> Non, merci. J'ai assez mangé.

> C'est bon ?

> Oui, c'est délicieux !

Who is saying what?

These little pictures show you different mealtime situations. Cover up the rest of the page and see if you know what everyone would say in French.

Simon is saying he is hungry.

The chef wants you to enjoy your meal.

Isabelle is saying "Help yourself".

Pierre wants someone to pass him a glass.

Maman is offering Simon more chips.

He says "Yes please" and that he likes chips.

Then he says "No thanks", he's had enough.

Marc is saying the food is delicious.

De

De often comes before **le**, **la** or **les** in French, as in **encore de** . . ? (some more . . ?). Before **le** and **les** it changes, as follows:

de + le = du	de + l' = de l'
de + la = de la	de + les = des

Your hobbies

These people are talking about their hobbies.

New words

faire	to do
faire de la peinture	to paint
faire la cuisine	to cook
le passe-temps	hobby
bricoler	to make things
danser	to dance
lire	to read
regarder la télé	to watch TV
tricoter	to knit
nager	to swim
jouer	to play
le sport	sport
le football	football
le tennis	tennis
la musique	music
écouter	to listen to
l'instrument (m)	instrument
le violon	violin
le piano	piano
le soir	in the evening

faire (to make or do)

je fais	I do
tu fais	you do
il/elle fait	he/she/it does
nous faisons	we do
vous faites	you do
ils/elles font	they do

jouer à and jouer de

When you talk about playing a sport, you say **jouer à**, then the name of the sport. **À + le** becomes **au**, e.g. **je joue au football** (I play football).

To talk about playing an instrument, you say **jouer de**. Remember that **de + le** becomes **du**, e.g. **je joue du piano** (I play the piano).

What do you do in the evenings?

The sporty type

Tu as des passe-temps ?

J'aime le sport !

Je nage,

je joue au football.

et je joue au tennis.

Music lovers

Vous avez des passe-temps ?

Oui, nous aimons écouter de la musique.

Vous jouez des instruments ?

Et, moi, je joue du piano.

Oui, moi, je joue du violon.

What are they doing?

A

B

C

D

E

Cover up the rest of the page and see if you can say what all these people are doing in

French, e.g. **Il joue au football**.
Can you say in French what your hobbies are?

Telling the time

Here you can find out how to tell the time in French. You can look up any numbers you don't know on page 40.

There is no word for "past" in French; you just add the number of minutes to the hour: **il est neuf heures cinq** (it is five past nine). To say "five to" you say **moins cinq** (less five): **il est neuf heures moins cinq** (it is five to nine).

New words

quelle heure est-il?	what is the time?
il est une heure	it is one o'clock
il est deux heures	it is two o'clock
moins cinq	five to
et quart	quarter past
moins le quart	quarter to
et demie*	half past
midi	midday
minuit	midnight
du matin	in the morning
du soir	in the evening
à	at
se lever	to get up
son	his/her
le petit déjeuner	breakfast
le déjeuner	lunch
le dîner	supper, dinner
il va	he goes
à l'école	to school
au lit	to bed

aller (to go)

je vais	I go
tu vas	you go
il/elle va	he/she goes
nous allons	we go
vous allez	you go (pl)
ils/elles vont	they go

What is the time?

Here is how to ask what the time is.

The time is …

Il est neuf heures cinq.

Il est neuf heures et quart.

Il est neuf heures et demie.

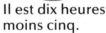

Il est dix heures moins le quart.

Il est dix heures moins cinq.

Il est midi/minuit.

What time of day?

Il est six heures du matin.

Il est six heures du soir.

26   *To say "half past twelve" you say **midi/minuit et demi.**

Marc's day

Read what Marc does throughout the day, then see if you can match each clock with the right picture. You can find out what the answers are on pages 44-45.

a b c d e f g h

1 Marc se lève à sept heures et demie.*

2 Il mange son petit déjeuner à huit heures.

3 A neuf heures moins le quart, il va à l'école.

4 Il mange son déjeuner à midi et demi.

5 A deux heures dix il joue au football.

6 A cinq heures et quart il regarde la télé.

7 A six heures il mange son dîner.

8 Il va au lit à huit heures et demie.

What time is it?

Can you say in French what times these clocks show?

a b c g h i k j l d e f m n o

*Some verbs are formed from two parts. You can read about these on pages 42-43.

Arranging things

Here is how to arrange things with your friends.

New words

on va . . ?	shall we go . . ?
quand?	when?
mardi	on Tuesday
le matin	in the morning
l'après-midi	in the afternoon
le soir	in the evening
la piscine	swimming pool
vers	at about
à mardi	until Tuesday
aujourd'hui	today
à demain	until tomorrow
ce soir	this evening
d'accord	O.K.
je ne peux pas	I can't
pas possible	that's no good
dommage	it's a pity!
aller à	to go to
le cinéma	cinema
la partie	party

Days of the week

dimanche	Sunday
lundi	Monday
mardi	Tuesday
mercredi	Wednesday
jeudi	Thursday
vendredi	Friday
samedi	Saturday

Tennis

Swimming

Going to the cinema

28

Going to a party

> Tu viens à ma partie?

> C'est quand?

> Samedi soir.

> Dommage. Pas possible.

> Samedi je vais danser.

Your diary for the week

Here is your diary, showing you what you are doing for a week. Read it, then see if you can answer the questions at the bottom of the page in French.

lundi
4 heures. Tennis.

mardi
2 heures. Piano.
5.30 Piscine.

mercredi
3 heures. Tennis.
7.45 Cinéma.

jeudi

Vendredi
8 heures. Danser avec Boris.

Samedi
2 heures. Football.
7 heures. Partie.

dimanche
Tennis l'après-midi.

Qu'est-ce que tu fais vendredi?
Quand joues-tu au tennis?
Tu vas quand au cinéma?
Tu joues du piano jeudi?
Qu'est-ce que tu fais dimanche?
A quelle heure est la partie samedi?

à + le

When **à** comes before **le**, you say **au** instead: **on va au cinema?** (shall we go to the cinema?)*

* You can find out more about this on pages 42-43.

Asking where places are

Here and on the next two pages you can find out how to ask your way around.

In French there are two words for "you" – **tu** and **vous***. You say **tu** to friends, but it is more polite to say **vous** when you talk to adults you don't know well.

New words

pardon	excuse me
je vous en prie	not at all
ici	here
là-bas	over there
la poste	post office
sur la place	in the market
du marché	place
l'hôtel	hotel
puis	then
tournez . .	turn . .
il y a . . ?	is there . . . ?
près d'ici	nearby
la rue	road, street
juste	just
c'est loin?	is it far?
à cinq minutes	five minutes away
à pied	on foot
le supermarché	supermarket
en face de	opposite
à côté de	next to
la banque	bank
la pharmacie	chemist's

Being polite

This is how to say "Excuse me". Always add **monsieur** or **madame**.

When people thank you, it is polite to answer **"Je vous en prie"**.

Where is . . . ?

Directions

tout droit

à gauche   **à droite**

 *See pages 42-43

Is there a . . . nearby?

Is it far?

Pardon, il y a un café près d'ici ?

Oui, juste à gauche dans la rue Racine.

C'est loin ?

Non, à cinq minutes à pied.

Pardon, il y a un supermarché près d'ici ?

Oui, là-bas en face de la banque.

Et il y a une pharmacie près d'ici ?

Juste à côté du supermarché.

Other useful places to ask for

la gare	une station service	les toilettes	une boîte aux lettres
the station	a petrol station	toilets	a letter box
une cabine téléphonique	un camping	l'hôpital	l'aéroport
a telephone box	a campsite	the hospital	airport

31

Finding your way around

Here you can find out how to ask your way around and follow directions. When you have read everything, try the map puzzle on the opposite page.

S il vous plaît is the polite way to say "please".

New words

pour aller à?	how do I get to?	**jusqu'à**	as far as
prenez . .	take . .	**en voiture**	by car
continuez . .	carry on . .	**la première rue**	the first street
l'auberge de		**la deuxième rue**	the second street
jeunesse (f)	youth hostel	**la troisième rue**	the third street
le syndicat		**l'Hôtel de Ville**	town hall
d'initiative	tourist office	**l'église(f)**	church

prendre	to take				
		nous prenons	we take	When people are telling you	
je prends	I take	**vous prenez**	you take	where to go, they use the	
tu prends	you take	**ils prennent**	they take(m)	**vous** part of the verb, e.g.	
il/elle prend	he/she takes	**elles prennent**	they take(f)	**Prenez la première rue** . . .	

Finding your way around Beauville

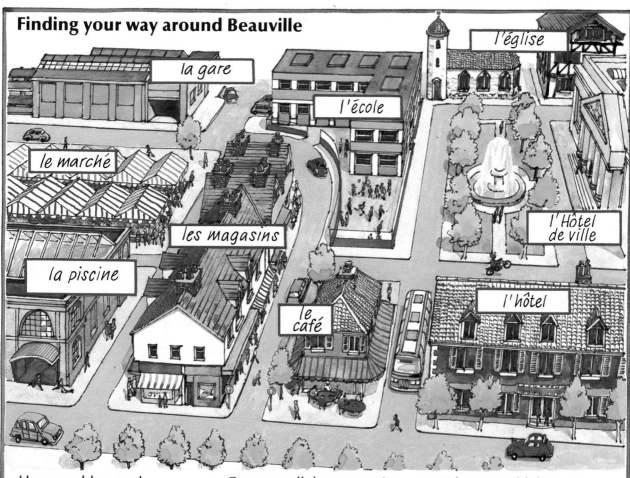

l'église
la gare
l'école
le marché
l'Hôtel de ville
les magasins
la piscine
l'hôtel
le café

How would you ask someone the way to the market place? How would you ask them if there is a café nearby? Ask how far it is.

Can you tell the person in the yellow car how to get to the church?
Can you direct someone from the hotel to the market?

Where would these directions take the yellow car?
Prenez la deuxième rue à gauche et c'est à droite.

Going shopping

Here and on the next two pages you can find out how to say what you want when you go shopping. When you go into a French shop you should say **"Bonjour, madame"** (or **monsieur**). If there are lots of people in there you say **"Bonjour, messieurs, mesdames"**.

Spending money

There are 100 **centimes** in a **euro**. On price labels, the symbol **€** is used after the price. For example, **deux euros** is written as **2€**, and **deux euros vingt** as **2,20€**. To understand prices you must know the numbers in French. They are listed on page 40.

New words

faire des courses	to go shopping
acheter	to buy
la boulangerie	baker's
l'épicerie(f)	grocer's
la boucherie	butcher's
le lait	milk
l'oeuf(m)	egg
le fruit	piece of fruit
le légume	vegetable
la viande	meat
le petit pain	bread roll
la pomme	apple
la tomate	tomato
vous désirez?	can I help you?
je voudrais	I would like
oui, bien sûr	with pleasure
c'est tout?	is that all?
et avec ça?	anything else?
ça fait combien?	how much is that?
voilà	there you are
un litre	a litre
un kilo	a kilo
une livre	half a kilo
alors	so, well then

Madame Delon goes shopping

Madame Delon fait des courses.

Elle achète du* pain à la boulangerie.

À la boulangerie

Bonjour, Madame.

Bonjour, Madame.

Je voudrais quatre petits pains.

Oui, bien sûr. C'est tout?

Trois euros, s'il vous plaît.

Oui, merci. Ça fait combien?

Voilà ! Merci !

*You can read about **du**, **de la** and **de l'** on page 21.

Internet links For links to websites where you can find lots of interactive lessons on going shopping, **go to** *www.usborne-quicklinks.com*

Elle achète du lait et des oeufs à l'épicerie.

Elle achète des fruits et des légumes au marché.

Elle achète de la viande à la boucherie.

À l'épicerie

Vous désirez?

Six oeufs, s'il vous plaît.

Et avec ça, Madame?

Un litre de lait, s'il vous plaît.

Ça fait combien?

Ça fait deux euros vingt.

Au marché

Bonjour, Madame. Vous désirez?

Un kilo de pommes, s'il vous plaît.

Et avec ça?

Une livre de tomates.

Alors, ça fait quatre euros.

More shopping and going to a café

Here you can find out how to ask how much things cost and how to order things in a café.

New words

coûter	to cost
combien coûte /coûtent?	how much is /are?
la carte postale	postcard
. . . le kilo	. . . a kilo
. . . la pièce	. . . each
la rose	rose
donnez m'en sept	give me seven
le café	coffee
l'addition(f)	the bill
le raisin	grape
l'orange(f)	orange
la banane	banana
l'ananas(m)	pineapple
le citron	lemon
la pêche	peach
la limonade	lemonade
le coca-cola	coca cola
le thé	tea
au lait	with milk
au citron	with lemon
le chocolat	hot chocolate
un verre de	a glass of
une glace	ice cream

Asking how much things cost

Combien coûte cette carte postale?

Soixante centimes.

Combien coûte le raisin?

Deux euros trente le kilo.

2,30€

Combien coûtent les roses?

Trois euros dix la pièce.

Alors, donnez-m'en sept, s'il vous plaît.

3,10€

Going to a café

Vous désirez?

Un café, s'il vous plaît.

Voilà!

Merci.

L'addition, s'il vous plaît.

Ça fait trois euros.

Buying fruit

Everything on the fruit stall is marked with its name and price.

Look at the picture, then see if you can answer the questions below it.

How do you tell the stallholder you would like four lemons, a kilo of bananas and a pineapple? How much do each of these things cost?

Qu'est-ce qui coûte deux euros la pièce?
Qu'est-ce qui coûte deux euros dix le kilo?
Qu'est-ce qui coûte deux euros trente le kilo?
Qu'est-ce qui coûte quarante centimes?

Things to order

Here are some things you might want to order in a café.

Je voudrais...

une limonade	un coca
un thé au lait	un thé au citron
un jus d'orange	un chocolat
un verre de lait	une glace

The months and seasons

Here you can learn what the seasons and months are called and find out how to say what the date is.

New words

le mois	month
l'année	year
quelle est la date?	what is the date?
aujourd'hui	today
l'anniversaire(m)	birthday

The seasons

le printemps	spring
l'été(m)	summer
l'automne(m)	autumn
l'hiver(m)	winter

The months

janvier	January
février	February
mars	March
avril	April
mai	May
juin	June
juillet	July
août	August
septembre	September
octobre	October
novembre	November
décembre	December

The seasons

le printemps

mars, avril, mai...

l'été

juin, juillet, août...

l'automne

septembre, octobre, novembre...

l'hiver

décembre, janvier, février

First, second, third . . .

For "first" you say **premier** for **le** words and **première** for **la** words. For "second" and so on you add **ième** to the number, e.g. **deuxième**. If the number ends in "e" you leave the "e" out, e.g. **quatrième** (fourth).*

With dates you say **le premier** for "the first", but for all the other dates you just say **le** plus the number.

Janvier est le premier mois de l'année.

Février est le deuxième mois de l'année.

Décembre est le douzième mois de l'année

Can you say where the rest of the months come in the year?

* **Neuf** (9) becomes **neuvième** (9th).

What is the date?

Aujourd'hui c'est le trois mai.

Quelle est la date aujourd'hui?

Le premier janvier.

Writing the date

Paris, le 3 mai.

Here you can see how a date is written. You put **le**, the number and the month. For "the first" you put **le 1er**.

When is your birthday?

C'est quand ton anniversaire?

C'est le dix novembre.

Mon anniversaire est le douze février.

L'anniversaire de Simon est le huit juin.

When are their birthdays?

The dates of the children's birthdays are written below their pictures. Can you say in French when they are, e.g. **L'anniversaire de Nicole est le deux avril**.

Nicole	Bertrand	Hélène	Claire	Claude	Roger
le 2 avril	le 21 juin	le 18 octobre	le 31 août	le 3 mars	le 7 septembre

39

Colours and numbers

Colours are describing words, so you add "e" when they refer to a **la** word, unless they end in 'e'. **Marron** does not change and **blanc** becomes **blanche**.

Internet links For links to websites with lots of online games on colours and numbers, go to www.usborne-quicklinks.com

The colours

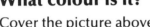

rouge bleu(e) jaune vert(e) orange rose noir(e) blanc(he) gris(e) marron

What colour is it?

Cover the picture above and see if you can say what colour everything is in the painting. You should know all the words you need.*

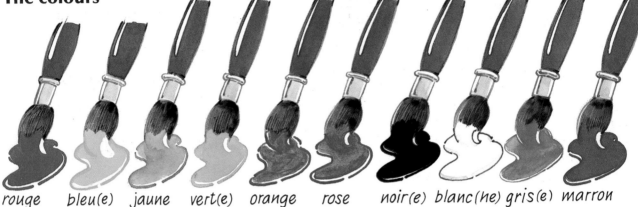

Numbers

You count the 30s, 40s, 50s, 60s and 80s in the same way as 20-29. For 70-79 you add 10-19 to **soixante** (60) and for 90-99 you add 10-19 to **quatre-vingts** (80).

1	un	11	onze	21	vingt et un	40	quarante
2	deux	12	douze	22	vingt-deux	50	cinquante
3	trois	13	treize	23	vingt-trois	60	soixante
4	quatre	14	quatorze	24	vingt-quatre	70	soixante-dix
5	cinq	15	quinze	25	vingt-cinq	71	soixante et onze
6	six	16	seize	26	vingt-six	80	quatre-vingts
7	sept	17	dix-sept	27	vingt-sept	81	quatre-vingt-un
8	huit	18	dix-huit	28	vingt-huit	90	quatre-vingt-dix
9	neuf	19	dix-neuf	29	vingt-neuf	91	quatre-vingt-onze
10	dix	20	vingt	30	trente	100	cent

*"The sky" is **le ciel**.

Pronunciation Guide

Internet links For links to websites where you can listen to examples of French pronunciation and try some French tongue-twisters, go to www.usborne-quicklinks.com

In French many letters are pronounced differently from in English. The best way to learn to speak French is to listen carefully to French people and copy what they say, but here are some general points to help you.

Below is a list of letters, with a guide to how to pronounce each one. For each French sound we have shown an English word, or part of a word, which sounds like it. Read it out loud in a normal way to find out how to pronounce the French sound, then practise saying the examples shown beneath.

a — Often like the "a" sound in "cat": **arriver, Paris, chat, mari**

e — Like the "a" sound in "above": **le, petit, regarder**

é — Like the "ay" sound in "late": **été, café, thé**

ê — Like the "a" sound in "care": **même, vous êtes**

i — Like the "i" in "machine": **il, dix, police, ville**

o — Like the "o" in "holiday": **fromage, pomme**

u — Round your lips as if to say "oo", then try to say "ee": **du, une, plus, musique**

eau, au — Like the "oa" sound in "toast": **eau, beau, gauche, château**

eu — Like the "u" sound in "fur": **deux, bleu, cheveux**

ou — Like the "oo" sound in "food": **ou, tout, beaucoup**

oi — Like the "wa" sound in "whack": **voix, poisson, boîte**

on, an, — Like "ong" without the "g" sound at the end: **dans, bonjour, français, Avignon**

un — Like the "u" sound in "sun". You do not pronounce the "n": **un, chacun**

in, ain, im — Like the "an" sound in "rang" without the "g" at the end: **vin, prince, impossible, train**

c — Before "i" or "e" it sounds like the "s" in "sun": **merci, France, certain**

Before other letters it sounds like the "c" in "cat": **café, coton, crabe**

ç — Like the "s" in "sun": **garçon, français**

ch — Like the "sh" sound in "shirt": **cochon, vache, chanter, Charles**

g — Before "i" or "e" it sounds like the "s" sound in "measure": **gendarme, girafe, âge**

Before other letters it is like the "g" in "get": **grand, gare, guitare**

gn — Like the "ni" sound in "onion": **campagne, montagne**

j — Like the soft "g" in girafe above: **bonjour, jeune**

th — Like the "t" in "top": **thé, théâtre**

qu — Like the "k" sound in "kettle": **question, musique**

h — This is not pronounced: **histoire, hôpital, hôtel**

A consonant at the end of a French word is not usually pronounced: **français, petit, les, tout.**

41

Grammar

Internet links For links to websites where you can conjugate French verbs online and find an online guide to French grammar, **go to www.usborne-quicklinks.com**

Grammar is like a set of rules about how you put words together and it is different for every language. You will find French easier if you learn some of its grammar, but don't worry if you don't understand all of it straightaway. Just read a little about it at a time. This is a summary of the grammar used in this book.

le, la, l'

In French every noun is masculine (m) or feminine (f). The word you use for "the" shows whether the noun is masculine or feminine and whether singular or plural. The word for "the" is **le** before masculine nouns, **la** before feminine nouns and **l'** before nouns beginning with a vowel:

le livre	the book
la maison	the house
l'arbre (m)	the tree

les

When you are talking about more than one thing the word for "the" is always **les**:

les livres	the books
les maisons	the houses
les arbres	the trees

You add "s" to most nouns to make the plural, but you don't pronounce it. Some plurals are formed differently and they are shown in brackets in the glossary on page 46.

au, aux

If **le** comes after **à**, they join together and become **au**:

Il est au cinéma   He is at the cinema.

à + les becomes **aux**:

la tarte aux fruits   fruit tart

du, des

If **le** comes after **de**, they join together and become **du**:

le prix du pain   the price of the bread

de + les becomes **des**:

le prix des oeufs   the price of the eggs

un, une

The word for "a" or "an" is **un** before masculine nouns and **une** before feminine nouns:

un livre	a book
une maison	a house
un arbre	a tree

some, any

The word for "some" or "any" is **du** before **le** words, **de la** before **la** words, **de l'** before nouns beginning with a vowel and **des** before plurals. The French often say "some" where there is nothing in English:

Il mange du pain.   He is eating bread.

Adjectives

An adjective is a describing word. French adjectives change their endings depending on whether they are describing a masculine or feminine word, and whether the word is singular or plural. In the word lists the masculine singular adjective is shown. You usually add "e" to this to make it feminine, unless it already ends in "e":

il est petit	he is small
elle est petite	she is small

You usually add "s" to an adjective to make it plural:

ils sont petits	they (m) are small
elles sont petites	they (f) are small

My, your

The word for "my" or "your" depends on whether the word that follows it is masculine or feminine, singular or plural:

mon/ton livre	my/your book
ma/ta maison	my/your house
mes/tes frères	my/your brothers

Pronouns

There are two words for "you" in French: **tu** and **vous**. You say **tu** to friends and **vous** when you want to be polite, or when you are talking to someone you don't know well, or more than one person. There are two words for "it": **il** for le words and **elle** for **la** words. There are also two words for "they": **ils** for boys, men and **le** words and **elles** for girls, women and **la** words. For masculine and feminine things together, you say **ils**.

I	**je**	he/it (m)	**il**	we	**nous**	they (m)	**ils**
you	**tu**	she/it (f)	**elle**	you	**vous**	they (f)	**elles**

Verbs

French verbs (doing words) change according to who is doing the action. Most of them follow regular patterns and have the same endings. The main type of verb used in this book ends in **er**, like **manger** (to eat). You can see what the different endings are on the right. There are some verbs in this book which do not follow this pattern, e.g. **avoir**, **être** and **aller**. It is best to learn them as you go along.

manger	to eat
je mange	I eat
tu manges	you eat
il/elle mange	he/she/it eats
nous mangeons	we eat
vous mangez	you eat
ils/elles mangent	they eat

Ne . . . pas

To make a verb negative in French, e.g. to say "I do not . . .", "he does not . . ." etc., you put **ne** immediately before the verb and **pas** immediately after it. **Ne** becomes **n'** if the verb begins with a vowel:

Je ne parle pas français.
I do not speak French.

Il n'aime pas le jambon.
He does not like ham.

Reflexive verbs

These are verbs which always have a special pronoun in front of them. Where in English we say "I get up", the French say "I get myself up". The pronoun changes according to who is doing the action, but **me** always goes with **je** and **te** with **tu** etc., as you can see on the right. **Me** becomes **m'** and **te** becomes **t'** if the verb begins with a vowel: **je m'appelle** (I am called), **tu t'appelles** (you are called).

se lever	to get up
je me lève	I get up
tu te lèves	you get up
il/elle se lève	he/she/it gets up
nous nous levons	we get up
vous vous levez	you get up
ils/elles se lèvent	they get up

Answers to puzzles

p.5

How are you?

The two people on the far right.

p.7

What are they called?

Il s'appelle Pierre.
Elle s'appelle Marie.
Ils s'appellent Paul et Jean.
Je m'appelle (your name).

Who is who?

Michel is talking to Jean.
Anne is talking to Pascale.
Michel is next to the seal.
Jean is talking to him.
Anne is in the bottom left-hand corner.
The man talking to Nicolas is going home.

Can you remember?

Comment tu t'appelles?
Je m'appelle . . .
C'est mon amie. Elle s'appelle Pascale.
Mon ami s'appelle Daniel.

p.9

Can you remember?

la/une fleur, le/un chat, l'/un arbre, le/un nid,
l'/un oiseau, le/un toit, le soleil, la/une fenêtre,
la/une voiture, le/un chien

p.11

Who comes from where?

Franz comes from Austria.
They are called Hari and Indira.
Lolita is Spanish.
Yes, Angus comes from Scotland.
Marie and Pierre come from France.
Yuri lives in Budapest.
Budapest is in Hungary.

Can you remember?

Tu viens d'où?   Je viens de . . .
Je parle français.   Tu parles français?

p.13

How old are they?

Michel is 13. Diane and Sylvie are 15. Guy is 12.
Odile is 11. Luc is 9. Colette is 5.

How many brothers and sisters?

A = Diane et Sylvie. B = Luc. C = Michel.
D = Guy. E = Odile.

p.17

Where is everyone?

Simon est dans la cuisine.
Pépé est dans la salle à manger.
Maman est dans la chambre.
Pierre est dans la salle de bains.
Isabelle est en haut.
Le fantôme est dans la chambre d'Isabelle.
Mémé est dans le salon.

Pépé. Simon. Pierre. Maman.

Dans le salon.
Dans la chambre d'Isabelle.
Dans la salle à manger.
Dans la salle de bains.

Can you remember?

Tu habites où?
Tu habites une maison ou un appartement?
à la campagne
en ville
Je suis en haut.
Je suis dans la cuisine.

p.19

Where are they hiding?

Le hamster est dans le vase.
Le petit chat est derrière la télévision.
Le petit chien est dans le placard.
La perruche est sur le rayon.
Le serpent est derrière le canapé.
La tortue est à côté du téléphone.

p.21

Who likes what?

1. Boris. 2. Jean. 3. Pépé.

p.23

Who is saying what?

"J'ai faim."
"Bon appétit."
"Sers-toi."
"Peux-tu me passer un verre?"
"Veux-tu encore des pommes frites?"
"Oui, merci. J'aime les pommes frites."
"Non, merci. J'ai assez mangé."
"C'est délicieux."

p.25

What are they doing?

A Il fait la cuisine. B Il nage. C Ils dansent.
D Elle joue du violon. E Il fait de la peinture.

p.27

Marc's day

1b, 2e, 3f, 4a, 5h, 6g, 7d, 8c.

What time is it?

A Il est trois heures cinq.
B Il est onze heures cinq.
C Il est neuf heures moins dix.
D Il est quatre heures moins le quart.
E Il est trois heures vingt-cinq.
F Il est sept heures et demie.
G Il est trois heures.
H Il est quatre heures.
I   Il est neuf heures.
J   Il est une heure et demie.
K Il est sept heures cinq.
L Il est dix heures et demie.
M Il est six heures.
N Il est quatre heures moins vingt-cinq.
O Il est deux heures moins cinq.

p.29

Vendredi soir je vais danser avec Boris.
Je joue au tennis lundi, mercredi et dimanche.

Je vais au cinéma mercredi soir.
Non, je joue du piano mardi.
Dimanche après-midi je joue au tennis.
Elle est à sept heures.

p.33

Pour aller à la place du marché, s'il vous plaît?
Pardon, il y a un café près d'ici?
C'est loin?

Prenez la troisième à gauche, puis allez tout droit.

Prenez la troisième à droite, puis allez tout droit. Le marché est à gauche.

To the school.

p.37

Je voudrais quatre citrons, un kilo de bananes et un ananas.
Quatre citrons coûtent un euro soixante.
Un kilo de bananes coûte un euro soixante-dix.
Un ananas coûte deux euros.

un ananas. les pêches. le raisin. un citron.

p.39

L'anniversaire de Bertrand est le vingt et un juin.
L'anniversaire d'Hélène est le dix-huit octobre.
L'anniversaire de Claire est le trente et un août.
L'anniversaire de Claude est le trois mars.
L'anniversaire de Roger est le sept septembre.

p.40

La rue est grise.
Le soleil est jaune.
Le toit est orange.
Le ciel est bleu.
Les fleurs sont roses.
Le chien est marron.
L'oiseau est noir.
La voiture est rouge.
Les arbres sont verts.
La maison est blanche.

Glossary

Adjectives are shown in their masculine singular form. You just add "e" to make them feminine. The feminine form is only shown as well when it is different from usual. Irregular plurals are shown in brackets next to the letters "pl".

à	at, to
à bientôt	see you soon
à côté de	next to
à droite	on the right
à gauche	on the left
à la campagne	in the country
à peu près	about
à pied	on foot
acheter	to buy
l'addition (f)	bill
affectueux, affectueuse	friendly
l'Afrique (f)	Africa
aimer	to like
l'Allemagne (f)	Germany
allemand	German
aller	to go
alors	then
l'ami (m), l'amie (f)	friend
l'ananas (m)	pineapple
anglais	English
l'Angleterre (f)	England
l'année (f)	year
l'anniversaire (m)	birthday
août	August
l'appartement (m)	flat
l'après-midi (m)	afternoon
l'arbre (m)	tree
l'armoire (f)	wardrobe
assez	enough, quite
l'auberge (f) de la jeunesse	youth hostel
au bord de la mer	by the sea
aujourd'hui	today
au revoir	Goodbye
aussi	also, too
l'automne (m)	autumn
l'Autriche (f)	Austria
avec	with
avoir	to have
avoir . . . ans	to be . . . years old
avoir faim	to be hungry
avril	April
la banane	banana
la banque	bank
la barrière	fence
beaucoup	a lot, much, many
le beurre	butter
bien	good, well
bien sûr	of course
le bifteck	steak
blanc, blanche	white
bleu	blue
blond	blond
la boîte aux lettres	post box
bon appétit!	Enjoy your meal!
bonjour	Hello
bonne nuit	Good Night
bonsoir	Good Evening
la boucherie	butcher's
la boulangerie	baker's
bricoler	to make things
brun	dark-haired
la cabine téléphonique	telephone box
le café	café
le camping	campsite
le canapé	sofa
la carte postale	postcard
ça va ?	how are you?
ce, cette	this, that
le château (pl. châteaux)	castle
la chambre	bedroom
le chat	cat
la cheminée	chimney
chercher	to look for
le chien	dog
le chocolat	chocolate
le ciel	sky
le cinéma	cinema
le citron	lemon
le coca-cola	coca-cola
combien?	how much?
comment tu t'appelles?	what is your name?
coûter	to cost
la cuisine	kitchen
d'accord	O.K.
dans	in
danser	to dance
décembre	December
le déjeuner	lunch
de l'après-midi	in the afternoon
demain	tomorrow
derrière	behind
deuxième	second
devant	in front of
dimanche	Sunday
le dîner	supper, dinner
dommage!	it's a pity!
d'où?	from where?
du matin	in the morning
du soir	in the evening
l'eau (f)	water
l'école (f)	school
l'Ecosse (f)	Scotland
écouter de	to listen to
encore de . . .	more . . .
en face de	opposite
en français	in French
en haut	upstairs
entre	between
en ville	in the town

en voiture	by car	la	the
l'épicerie (f)	grocer's	là-bas	over there
l'Espagne (f)	Spain	le	the
et	and	le lait	milk
l'été (m)	summer	le légume	vegetable
être	to be	le mieux	best
		la limonade	lemonade
faire	to make, do	lire	to read
faire de la peinture	to paint	le lit	bed
faire des courses	to go shopping	le litre	litre
faire la cuisine	to cook	la livre	half a kilo
la famille	family	le livre	book
le fantôme	ghost	loin	far
le fauteuil	armchair	lundi	Monday
la fenêtre	window		
février	February	madame	Mrs.
la fleur	flower	mademoiselle	Miss
le football	football	mai	May
le franc	franc	mais	but
français	French	la maison	house
la France	France	mal	badly
le frère	brother	maman	Mum
le fromage	cheese	manger	to eat
le fruit	fruit	le marché	market
		mardi	Tuesday
le garage	garage	marron	brown
la gare	station	mars	March
le gâteau (pl.gâteaux)	cake	le matin	morning
la glace	ice-cream	mémé	Granny
grand	tall	merci	thank you
la grand-mère	grandmother	mercredi	Wednesday
les grands-parents	grandparents	la mère	mother
le grand-père	grandfather	midi	midday, noon
gris	grey	mieux	better
gros, grosse	fat	mince	thin
		minuit	midnight
habiter	to live	la minute	minute
le hamburger	hamburger	moi	me
le hamster	hamster	moins	less
l'hiver (m)	winter	le mois	month
la Hongrie	Hungary	mon, ma, mes	my
l'hôtel (m)	hotel	monsieur	Mr., sir
ici	here	nager	to swim
l'Inde (f)	India	le nid	nest
il n'y a pas de quoi	not at all	noir	black
il y a	there is, there are	non	no
		novembre	November
le jambon	ham		
janvier	January	octobre	October
jaune	yellow	l'oeuf (m)	egg
jeudi	Thursday	l'oncle (m)	uncle
jeune	young	l'oiseau (m) (pl.oiseaux)	bird
je vous en prie	don't mention it	orange	orange
jouer	to play	l'orange (f)	orange (fruit)
juillet	July	ou	or
juin	June	où?	where?
le jus d'orange	orange juice	oui	yes
jusqu'à	as far as		
		le pain	bread
le kilo	kilo	papa	Dad

47

pardon	excuse me	samedi	Saturday
les parents	parents	la saucisse	sausage
parler	to speak	se lever	to get up
pas du tout	not at all	le serpent	snake
pas possible	that's no good	s'il te plaît	please
le passe-temps	hobby	s'il vous plaît	please (polite)
la pêche	peach	la soeur	sister
pépé	Grandad	le soleil	sun
le père	father	le soir	evening
la perruche	budgie	son, sa, ses	his, her, its
petit	small	sous	under
le petit chat	kitten	les spaghetti (m. pl.)	spaghetti
le petit chien	puppy	le sport	sport
le petit déjeuner	breakfast	la station service	petrol station
le petit pain	bread roll	le supermarché	supermarket
la pharmacie	chemist's	sur	on top of
le piano	piano	le syndicat d'initiative	tourist office
la pièce	each (one)		
la pizza	pizza	la table	table
le placard	cupboard	la tante	aunt
la place du marché	market place	le tapis	carpet
la plante	plant	la tarte aux fruits	fruit tart
le poisson	fish	le téléphone	telephone
la pomme	apple	la télévision	television
les pommes frites	chips	le tennis	tennis
la porte	door	le thé	tea
la poste	post office	le toit	roof
premier, première	first	la toilette	toilet
prendre	to take	la tomate	tomato
près d'ici	nearby	ton, ta, tes	your (sing.)
presque	almost	toujours	always
le printemps	spring	tourner	to turn
puis	then	tout droit	straight ahead
		la tortue	tortoise
quand?	when?	très	very
quel, quelle	what	tricoter	to knit
quelque chose	something	troisième	third
qui?	who?	trouver	to find
la quiche	quiche		
		un, une	a, an
le raisin	grape		
le rayon	bookshelf	le vase	vase
regarder	to watch	vendre	to sell
le rideau	curtain	vendredi	Friday
le riz	rice	venir de	to come from
rose	pink	le verre	glass
la rose	rose	vert	green
rouge	red	le vestibule	hall
la rue	street	veux-tu . . . ?	would you like . . . ?
		la viande	meat
la salade	salad	vieux, vieille	old
la salle à manger	dining room	le violon	violin
la salle de bains	bathroom	voici!	here is . . . !
le salon	living room	voilà!	there is . . . !
Salut!	Hi!, Hello	la voiture	car

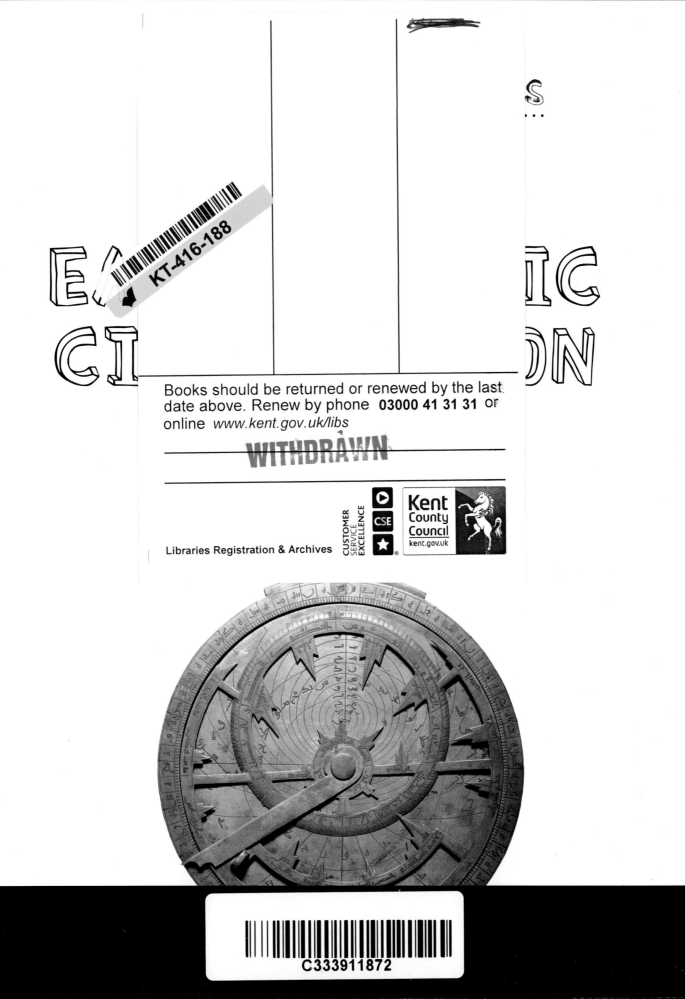

Books should be returned or renewed by the last date above. Renew by phone **03000 41 31 31** or online *www.kent.gov.uk/libs*

Franklin Watts
Published in Great Britain in 2016 by The Watts Publishing Group

Copyright © Franklin Watts 2014

Editor in Chief: John C. Miles
Editor: Sarah Ridley
Art director: Peter Scoulding
Series designer: John Christopher/White Design
Picture research: Diana Morris

A CIP catalogue record for the book is available from the British Library.

Dewey number: 956

ISBN 978 1 4451 3410 9

Printed in China

Franklin Watts
An imprint of
Hachette Children's Group
Part of The Watts Publishing Group
Carmelite House
50 Victoria Embankment
London EC4Y 0DZ

An Hachette UK Company
www.hachette.co.uk

www.franklinwatts.co.uk

Picture credits
Paul Cowan/Shutterstock: 25. Dewberry 77/Dreamstime: 23. Bequest of Joseph H Durkee/
Metropolitan Museum of Art, New York: 14. Dziewul/Shutterstock: 15. Oliver Goujon/
Robert Harding PL: 10. Homedesmarc/Dreamstime: 5. Iberfoto/Superstock: front
cover, 1, 17. Images & Stories/Alamy: 29. Lukasz Kasperek/Dreamstime: 16. Marko5/
Dreamstime: 13. Metropolitan Museum of Art, New York: 6. Oronoz/Album/Superstock:
24. Photogenes: 19, 21. David Poole/Robert Harding PL: 7. Paull Randt: 28.
Louie Schoeman/Dreamstime: 12. Sotheby's: 18, 22. Jean Soutif/Look at Sciences/SPL: 9.
Suronin/Dreamstime: 20. Guy Thouvenin/Robert Harding PL: 8.
Ufukguler/Dreamstime: 27. Nik Wheeler/Alamy: 11.
Zereshk/Wikipedia: 26.

*In this book, we have used the abbreviation pbuh (peace be upon him) when mentioning the
name of the Prophet Muhammad (pbuh) to show respect.*

CONTENTS

WHERE DID IT ALL BEGIN?

In 632 CE the Holy Prophet Muhammad (pbuh) died in Madinah, a desert city in Saudi Arabia. The Prophet spent his life encouraging Arab tribes within his region to believe in one god, Allah. He also inspired them to love learning, discovery and creativity. After his death, his followers created the Islamic civilisation – one of the greatest in the world.

Mosques

It was important for all Muslims to construct a mosque wherever they settled. Here, Muslims could gather together to worship Allah, to learn, to discuss their faith and sort out community matters. The Prophet himself designed the first mosque near Madinah, from which all others take their main shape and purpose. The first mosques were open-air and made of sun-baked clay walls and palm trunks. A shaded courtyard space offered travellers and the sick a place of rest and recovery.

Islam in the Golden Age

After the Prophet's death, religious rulers called caliphs spread Islam far and wide. These caliphs ruled over realms called caliphates. The first was run by the Umayyads, whose capital was Damascus in Syria. They established Islamic territories as far west as North Africa, Sicily and Spain. But by 750 a second caliphate became dominant. This was ruled by the Abbasids, whose capital was Baghdad in Iraq. Under their leadership it became the glistening cultural heart of Islam.

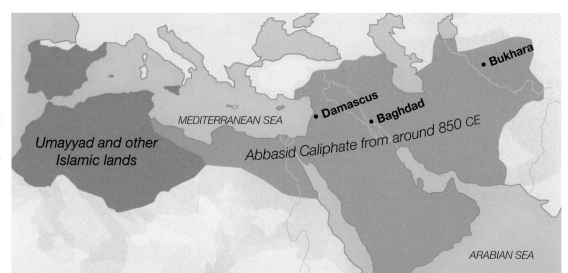

This map shows the rough extent of the Abbasid Caliphate and other Islamic lands from around the mid-800s CE – modern-day countries covered by this map area include Iran, Iraq, Syria, Jordan, Saudi Arabia, Egypt, Tunisia, Morocco, Spain and Portugal.

Bukhara

MEDITERRANEAN SEA

Damascus

Baghdad

Umayyad and other Islamic lands

Abbasid Caliphate from around 850 CE

ARABIAN SEA

The Dome of the Rock in Jerusalem was built in 691 CE and is the oldest surviving mosque. It was built on the rock from which Prophet Muhammad (pbuh) ascended to heaven to receive messages from Allah.

The evidence

How do we know about Islamic civilisation in the first three centuries after the death of the Prophet? We know a lot from written texts and inscriptions made on artefacts and architectural features. Under Islam, the Arabic alphabet and script developed to record the life and teachings of the Prophet. Later, Arabic was used for writing poetry, scientific research and discoveries, histories, travels and trade.

Around the world

c. 3000–1460 BCE Pakistan/India
Archaeology tells us about the Indus Valley's great cities such as Mohenjo-Daro and Harappa. But for the moment we know nothing about the first rulers.

c. 3000–30 BCE Egypt
Archaeology and hieroglyphs tell us about ancient Egypt. Pharaoh Namer was the first king of a united Egypt around 3000 BCE.

900 CE West Africa
We know about the origin of the Kingdom of Benin through archaeology and oral, or spoken, history. Ogiso Igodo was the first Ogiso, or king.

5

WARFARE AND WEAPONS

The first Islamic military campaigns after the Prophet's death were waged by his father-in-law, Caliph Abu-Bakr. Foot soldiers and horse or camel cavalries then expanded the Islamic empire through Arab lands and far beyond.

Weapons of style

Islamic armies were well organised by trusted generals, who were given large territories to administer once they had been conquered. Early Islamic generals fought firstly with a mix of familiar, local weapons. Later, Islamic weaponry developed its own identity. It was lightweight, strong and lethal. It included razor-sharp sabres, daggers, maces, cutlasses and axes, with stylish, highly decorated handles.

This long, slender sword with its hilt (handle) of gold, silver, ivory, pearls, rubies and turquoises is from the 15th century. But it resembles the lethal shape of earlier Muslim weapons.

Cutting edge

Skill with the bow and arrow was highly prized, especially when archers fired their arrows from a galloping horse. This particular skill improved even further when Turkish slave soldiers arrived. The Abbasids brought in these excellent horsemen to help defend the caliphate. It was a decision that they were later to regret (see pages 28-29).

Early Islamic caliphs and generals built strong fortresses to defend their territories. This one, at Arg-é-Bam in modern-day Iran, was destroyed by an earthquake in 2003.

Deadly beauty

The power of early Islamic weaponry lay in its materials. The Syrian city of Damascus was famed for the steel used to make swords and daggers. 'Damascus steel' or 'watered steel' was prized in Europe for its strength and sharpness. Its wavy pattern was a sign of its quality and durability. The effect was created during the smelting process in crucibles, which were white-hot earthenware ovens.

 Around the world

c. 3000–30 BCE Egypt
Pharaohs have great stocks of weapons. Some of these are copied from their captured enemies. The khopesh – a thick, curved sword – is horribly effective.

c. 1600–1460 BCE China
Shang Dynasty armies fight with bronze weapons and fast-moving horse-drawn chariots.

c. 900 CE Central America
Mayan kingdoms fight wars with each other using stone clubs and arrows with tips made from glass-like obsidian. Sometimes Mayans resolve conflicts through 'peace talking'.

ORDER AND ORGANISATION

By the mid 700s, the Abbasid caliphs had stamped their power across a wide region. All they needed now was a capital city from which to run it. It was important for them to build something grand — a symbol of central power and tight organisation.

This reconstruction artwork shows the walls around 10th-century Baghdad. Each ring of walls could be defended separately.

Building Baghdad

The Abbasid Caliph, al-Mansur, rejected the Umayyads' capital, Damascus. In 763, he chose instead to build Baghdad on a flat site on the great River Tigris, in modern-day Iraq. It was well placed along existing trade routes and its climate was healthy. Over 100,000 architects, builders and craftsmen worked on the city. They came from all over the Muslim world and from different faiths. Abbasid caliphs encouraged this diversity.

Strength and power

Baghdad was also known as *Madinat al Salam*, the 'city of peace'. But it was designed to draw the eye to the strong power base at its centre. To this end, it was planned in three rings, with a huge mosque and the caliph's palace at its heart. Two broad avenues linked four massive gates, and a moat surrounded it. Outside the city's core, bustling markets and industries indicated the city's commercial importance.

Cutting edge

Caliph al-Mansur ruled the Abbasid Empire firmly, and according to strict Islamic law. This law covered everything from family matters and land disputes to taxation. But al-Mansur broke away from earlier rulers' use of Arab administrators. Instead, he chose capable, well qualified men from across the empire. They became judges, advisors, ambassadors, generals and wazirs. A huge network of clerks and officials supported their work.

9

Around the world

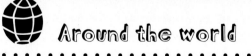

c. 3000–1460 BCE Indus Valley
Indus Valley cities are built of baked clay. Their grandest buildings and widest streets are often set up high on mounds. Narrower streets lie below.

900 CE Kingdom of Benin
The king's palace is surrounded by a thick clay and wood wall and a deep ditch. This, and the whole city, lie within an outer wall and strong gates.

900 CE Central America
The Mayans build grand cities, palaces and temples from large, shaped stone blocks. Amazingly, they use only stone or flint tools to cut and chisel them.

LIFE IN BAGHDAD

Baghdad was well known for its splendid buildings made from large blocks of marble and stone. Its streets contained houses with highly decorated balconies and roof terraces. This style is known as *Shanasheel*, which refers to the elaborate windows.

10

A city of skills

Further from Baghdad's centre, the streets narrowed. Clusters of kiln-baked and sun-baked brick buildings housed manufacturing industries. The city thronged with bakers, carvers, metalworkers, jewellers, leatherworkers and many other highly skilled artisans. They sold their goods in busy markets and organised themselves into associations called guilds, which kept standards high.

Beating the heat

Shanasheel windows were first recorded in Baghdad as late as the 1100s. However, the design had developed earlier in Islamic Spain, where skilled craftsmen pierced intricate patterns into wood or stone windows. These were often built on three sides, with a cushioned window seat inside, and a shelf for unglazed water pots. Breezes blowing through the pierced windows cooled both the water in the pots and the room.

There are still traditional shanasheel houses in Baghdad today. Their sunny balconies and latticed windows are often finely carved. Inside, there is a cool, private courtyard.

Cool place to be

Baghdad around 900 was an international city, much like London and New York are today. People were drawn to it from all over the caliphate. They enjoyed its wide streets fanning out from the centre and visited its shopping arcades filled with luxury goods. Busy government officials, scribes, translators and merchants wandered through peaceful watered parks and flower gardens.

A busy covered market, or bazaar, in Isfahan, Iran. Today bazaars are still a central feature of cities across the Islamic world.

Around the world

c. 3000–30 BCE Egypt
Artisans such as coppersmiths, goldsmiths, basket weavers, perfumiers and potters live in quarters on the edge of cities such as Memphis. Many work for the pharaoh.

c. 1600–1460 BCE China
Workshops for bronze workers, stonemasons, jade carvers and other artisans are built near the royal palace. The workers live in small houses nearby.

900 CE Kingdom of Benin
Each group of skilled bronze workers, wood and ivory carvers and cloth makers lives in their own quarters within the city walls. They are organised into guilds.

TRAVELLING ACROSS THE CALIPHATES

Travel was the lifeblood of the early Islamic Empire. Boats called dhows carried goods and passengers to ports around the Persian Gulf and East Africa, making long-distance journeys relatively easy. Meanwhile, caravans of heavily-laden camels criss-crossed desert sands.

12

This modern dhow is built to a traditional design, and is capable of carrying very heavy goods. It is shown cruising near Zanzibar, an important East African early Islamic trading port.

A thirst for travel

Roads and pathways from Persia to Spain were teeming with travellers on foot, horseback or on donkeys. These travellers included scholars, religious teachers, geographers, ambassadors and tourists as well as merchants. The Muslim tradition of hospitality meant that they were welcomed and given food and shelter along the way.

Cutting edge

Large dhows with crews of 30 were perfect for shipping trade goods along the eastern Indian Ocean and through the Red Sea. Wheeled carts were useless across the sands and rocks of the Arabian Desert and the Sahara but the camel was just perfect. Its broad feet easily coped with heavy loads and sinking sands.

Travel writing

Travel led to the first true tourism and travel writing. Wealthy tourists took part in a Grand Tour, a *Jawla*, and were given the respected title, *Jawwal*. At first, travellers narrated their accounts to spellbound audiences. Then, they became diaries that were included in the works of intrigued scientists. By 1100, the *rihla*, the first true travel writing, was published. Since then, great Muslim travel writers such as Ibn Battuta (1304-1377) have given us a window into the medieval Islamic world.

Camel caravans like this crossed the Sahara, where great Islamic trading settlements such as Sijilmasa emerged. The western trans-Saharan trade in salt, gold and leather was very valuable.

 ## Around the world

c. 3000–1460 BCE Indus Valley
Indus Valley settlements are built near the great Indus River, so many traders and travellers use boats. People walk or use carts over mountain passes.

c. 3000–30 BCE Egypt
Small boats made from papyrus and large wooden ships carry trade goods, travellers and the pharaoh's ambassadors. Pack animals such as camels are used across desert lands.

900 CE Kingdom of Benin
Benin's traders carry lightweight goods on their heads along a network of forest pathways. Large canoes transport heavier goods and soldiers along creeks and rivers.

WHERE TRADE GOES, ISLAM GOES

The gold coin below is a Syrian dinar. It dates from 698-699, and its inscription is in Arabic. The coin's date tells us that even in the first decades of Islam, Islamic trade was healthy. By the time of the Abbasids, trade networks had expanded across the now-vast Islamic lands.

14

A wealth of goods

For centuries before Islam, goods from as far as China had reached right across to Europe along the so-called Silk Road. In early Islamic times, caliphs controlled this trade as soon as it reached their territory. In Baghdad's shopping arcades, the wealthy could buy silk, linen, printed cloth, furs, precious metals and stones, spices and slaves.

Trade and faith

Each time this coin changed hands, the message of Islam was spread. Teachers of Islam often travelled with the caravans, too. Islam took hold along trade routes deep into the southern Sahara. It was known even as far as Scandinavia, where Muslim traders bought precious furs.

This Syrian gold dinar has the Muslim declaration of belief in Allah – the *Shahada* – inscribed on it. The inscription reads, 'There is no god but Allah and Muhammad is the messenger of Allah.'

This picture shows a caravanserai, a protective fortress and stopping point for Islamic merchants and travellers. Here, animals could be stabled and goods sold or bartered. This caravanserai is in Anatolia, Turkey.

Postal orders

A strong banking system developed among early Islamic trading nations. This meant that letters promising payment were honoured all the way from Baghdad in the East to Portugal in the West. The Abbasids also introduced a postal system that helped merchants to communicate with each other. But the Baghdadi caliphs used it as a spy network, which included spying on the merchants!

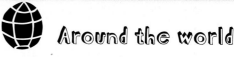

Around the world

c. 3000–30 BCE Egypt

Goods are bartered. But grain and oil are also used as a type of money. These can be stored and used in times of famine. Some peasants get rich on storing them.

900 CE Kingdom of Benin

Traders sell cloth, spices and elephant ivory and other goods to neighbouring kingdoms. Their currencies are cowrie shells and brass bracelets called manillas.

900 CE Central America

Mayans barter their cloth, pottery, feathers, ornaments, bells and precious stones such as jade. Their long trade routes link North and South America.

SCIENCE REACHES THE STARS

The elaborate brass object in the main picture is an Arabic astrolabe dating from the 900s. Astrolabes were used in both astronomy and astrology – just two of the many sciences studied by enthusiastic early Islamic scholars.

16

A thirst for knowledge

The quest for trade, travel and pure enlightenment thrust forward science, mathematics, geography and medicine during the early Islamic period. Scholars sought knowledge from China to India and from Persia to Spain. Baghdad became a great centre of learning. The city's 'House of Wisdom', completed by Caliph al-Ma'mun in 813, attracted scholars of all faiths.

A view inside the University of al-Qarawiyyan in Morocco, the first Islamic university. It was founded in 859 CE by Fatima al-Fihri, a Muslim woman dedicated to education.

Islamic Spain introduced the astrolabe and other navigational instruments to Christian European sailors, enabling them to find their way more accurately.

Cutting edge

The astrolabe could measure the universe in three dimensions. Together with the quadrant, it helped tell both time and distance. For Muslims, they also pinpointed the *quibla* – the direction of Makkah to which they prayed.

Star gazers

Developments in mathematics made new instruments far more accurate. Early Islamic mathematicians hugely improved algebra and trigonometry. This in turn pushed forward knowledge of time, space and distance. Mathematicians such as al-Battani (850-929) revolutionised *zijs*. These were numerical tables listing the positions and movement of the Sun, Moon and fixed stars, and coordinates within the solar system.

17

Around the world

c. 3000–30 BCE Egypt
Architects use a measuring rod to design huge pyramids. Farmers measure the Nile flood's depth with them. Mathematics and the decimal system are developed.

c. 1600–1460 BCE China
An early type of porcelain is invented during the Shang Dynasty, and other crafts such as bronze making advance greatly. Astronomers develop a calendar based on the cycles of the Moon.

900 CE Central America
Mayans develop complicated arithmetic of their own and understand the importance of 'zero'. They tell the time through the movements of the Moon, Venus and constellations.

FAITH WRITING

The page below from the Holy Qur'an shows the most important function of Arabic writing. This was to record the Word of Allah, as revealed by Archangel Gabriel to the Prophet. In Early Islamic states, Arabic became vital for trade, administration and learning.

Spreading the Word

The written Qur'an, and another set of writings called the Hadith, enabled all Muslims to understand and study their faith. During early Islamic times, Arabic was standardised. This meant that it had to be written using rules of grammar that everyone could learn. So teachers, scholars, traders, travellers, administrators or soldiers could communicate easily across the empire.

18

This page from the Qur'an was handwritten in the late 800s or early 900s.

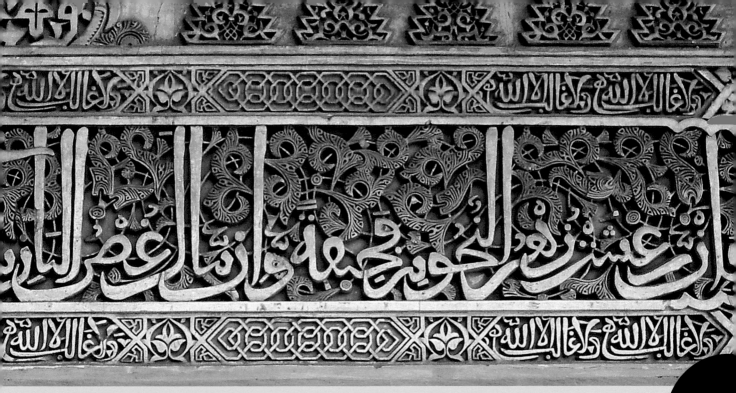

Craftsmen and artists used Arabic words and phrases to decorate pots, fabric and buildings, as here in the plasterwork of the Alhambra in Spain.

Beautiful and practical

Early Islamic scribes wrote in ink, watercolours and gold, and used pens rather than brushes. They worked on sheets of parchment, made from dried animal skins. Later, they adopted paper technology from ancient China, but refined the paper's texture with a coating of starch paste. Sometimes, writing surfaces were dyed with deep colours such as indigo blue. Gold lettering made a sparkling contrast.

Reading the script

Each line of the Holy Qur'an is read from right to left, with every page written in elegant Arabic script. The picture on the left-hand page shows the early Kufic style. There are many others, but they all show 28 different consonants. There are no symbols for different vowel sounds, but small dots indicate where vowels should be. Other dots help the reader to distinguish between consonants that look similar.

Around the world

c. 3000–30 BCE Egypt
Ancient Egyptians developed hieratic (cursive) writing and numerals, which were written by priests on papyrus and walls. Hieroglyphs (picture writing) uses picture forms as well as symbols.

c. 1600–1460 BCE China
Shang Dynasty writers inscribe symbols on bronze, and on oracle bones, which are used to predict the future. These early writings confirm what later writers say about the Shang Dynasty.

c. 900 CE Central America
The Mayans develop an advanced form of writing called Zapotec. It records flourishing farming and the profits from bustling trade. Mayans record their history, too.

WONDERFUL WATER

Islam spread from the deserts of Arabia to many other dry, rocky lands. So water was always precious and the desert oasis was seen as a green jewel in the sands. Early Islamic cities such as Baghdad were built or expanded along other natural waterways, such as rivers and hot springs.

Eram Garden in Shiraz, a city in Iran, was built in the mid 1800s but has many older design features. Eram comes from the Arabic *Iram*, which means 'heaven'.

20

Irrigating the crops

Water was essential for irrigating food crops, and Early Islamic engineers designed elaborate watercourses for farming. Baghdad was built along the wide River Tigris, so its citizens had a constant supply of water. But with a population that reached over half a million by 900, the city needed irrigation to grow crops on the nearby river floodplain's fertile soils. So Baghdad's engineers built a system of canals that ran along high banks. These canals also served as protective ramparts.

Tiling became popular in homes and mosques throughout the Islamic world in the 10th to 11th centuries. Patterns showed complex geometry, such as here, or beautiful floral and leaf patterns.

21

Gardens of paradise

Beautiful flower gardens with fountains and trickling streams were also important in early Islamic cities. These gardens were taken from descriptions of paradise gardens in the Holy Qur'an. But many were influenced by pre-Islamic Sasanian design. This featured a plot divided into four quarters by streams; each quarter was planted with flowers and shade trees.

Cutting edge

Islamic tiles like the ones shown above shine and shimmer in water. They lined the public and private bathhouses, or hammams. We do not know exactly when tiled bathhouses were first built. We do know that by the 800s, Baghdad alone had around 5,000 of them. Hammams hummed with workers, from the dung collectors who provided fuel to heat the water to stokers, water carriers, robe keepers and skilled barbers.

Around the world

c. 3000–1460 BCE Indus Valley
The great Indus River supplies endless water. Homes in the major cities have shower rooms where the water drains into large clay-pipe sewers.

c. 3000–30 BCE Egypt
The Nile floodwaters are drained into basins and then into canals. Machines such as the shaduf then irrigate the crops.

900 CE Kingdom of Benin
Large Benin houses have courtyards where rainwater runs into underwater storage systems. Water is purified in huge pottery jars using herbs.

A BURST OF FLAVOUR

The main picture shows a plate made for the table of a wealthy family. It represents the importance of dining well in early Islamic civilisations. At that time, Islamic scientists improved farming tools, irrigation and flour milling techniques used by other cultures. In this way, food production increased.

Celebrity chefs

Imported foods such as rice from India, sorghum from Africa, and fruits, vegetables, herbs and spices helped to create Baghdad's distinctive food tradition. We know a lot about the dishes enjoyed by the elite through Ibn Sayyar al-Warraq's book, *The Book of Cookery Preparing Salubrious Foods and Delectable Dishes*. It was written in about 950 but is a collection of recipes from the caliphs' kitchens in the 800s.

This glazed bowl dates from the 900s and comes from what is modern-day Iran. Later patterns were more complex and colourful.

A world of flavours

Early Islamic cooking gave us many flavours and recipes. Ibn Sayyar al-Warraq's recipe book included a carrot smoothie, flavoured with ginger and honey. Carrots were a favourite ingredient and came in reds, yellows and whites. They were used a lot in puddings, like khabis. This set custard was made with milk, honey, eggs and carrots, flavoured with cloves, nutmeg, ginger and cassia, which is like cinnamon.

Desert foods

The food culture of the desert, where Prophet Muhammad lived, remained important to Muslims. Meals of sheep, goats, milk, dates, figs, grapes, pomegranates, honey, barley and wheat bread were timeless ingredients for many. All Muslims are required to fast between sunrise and sunset during the month of Ramadan. The tradition of breaking the fast by eating three dates, was and still is, popular.

Dates are the fruit of the date palm, shown here. Dried dates were and still are an important desert food that gives energy. They can be easily transported without spoiling.

23

Around the world

c. 900 CE Central America
Mayans grow maize as their main crop. They also eat cactus, greens, beans, rabbit, turkey and fruits.

900 CE Kingdom of Benin
Benin lies in thick forest, where animals are hunted. Rivers and creeks provide fish, such as the mudfish. Yams are the staple crop.

c. 3000–1460 BCE Indus Valley
Farmers grow wheat that is made into flat bread. Most people eat grains, vegetables, salted sea fish, and river crocodile.

FINE FABRICS

The fabric fragment in the picture below is from a silk shawl, from about 900 CE. There is little written information on fabrics from this early period. But survivals like this show fine quality with vibrant colour and attractive design.

This beautifully woven silk shawl comes from the Islamic city of Cordoba, in Spain. Islamic Spain developed its own silk industry, so silk no longer had to imported from the Far East.

24

Islamic fabrics like these are made from camel hair and have long been used to keep nomadic traders and herders warm. They are richly patterned with natural dyes.

Magic carpets

Baghdad had such a large population that it had to import thousands of rugs and carpets from eastern Persia. Some designers continued the early Sasanian tradition of dividing the rug's pattern into four quarters, rather like their gardens. But newer Islamic motifs such as the crescent moon, star, flowers, fruits and vegetables were applied.

A world of cloth

Many early Islamic cloth fragments have been found in Egypt, Yemen and elsewhere, but they were most likely made in Baghdad. Fabrics include a surprising mix of linen, cotton and rabbit fur. Others are plain linen, or linen and wool mix. They are painted or stamped with repeated wood-block patterns, or panels of Arabic script.

25

Fashion divide
There were differences in fashion between East and West; between the Abbasids of Baghdad and the Umayyads of Sicily, Spain and North Africa. But generally, men and women wore plain or patterned long tunics over wide trousers. Long shawls or hooded cloaks covered women's shoulders and sometimes their heads, while men wore a turban or a close-fitting cap. Fine filigree gold and silver jewellery were prized accessories.

🌐 Around the world

c. 3000–30 BCE Egypt
Egyptians grow flax along the banks of the River Nile. It is woven into long, white, lightweight strips of linen cloth. Pigments from earth and rocks dye cloth for the rich.

c. 900 CE Central America
Mayans weave material from bark, cotton and the hemp plant. They embroider animal symbols such as the snake, and long bands showing the stars and planets.

900 CE Kingdom of Benin
Benin is famous for its cotton cloth, dyed with natural pigments. Women weavers make it in different thicknesses and in plain, striped or more complex chequered patterns.

PLEASURE AND LEISURE

Islamic instrument makers developed the *oud*, or lute – the stringed instrument in the main picture. Composers set poetry to music, creating unique musical forms. These songs were made to entertain the wealthy. But music and other pastimes spread to the streets right across the Islamic world.

26 Pastimes for princes

The horse was ridden for pleasure as well as battle, so Baghdad's elite took up the ancient Persian game of polo. A 10th century historian, Dinvari, wrote that 'a player should strictly avoid using strong language and should be patient and temperate'. These qualities meant that polo, as well as music, backgammon and a form of chess called *shatranj* were all part of a wealthy boy's education.

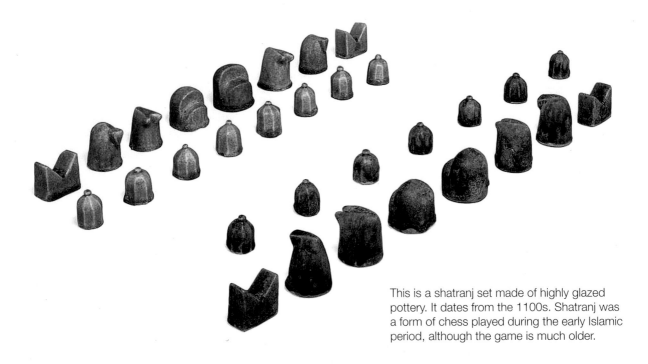

This is a shatranj set made of highly glazed pottery. It dates from the 1100s. Shatranj was a form of chess played during the early Islamic period, although the game is much older.

Instrument makers developed the oud, shown here, flute, bass drum, guitar, sitar, early violin, castanet, and others. These were based on earlier Arabic instruments.

Mixing the music

Classical Islamic music developed from older Arab, Persian and Byzantine styles, with influences from Africa, too. The music of the desert fused with urban music to produce new sounds, and Baghdad became a centre for this new kind of music. Islamic musicians wrote books of song and musical theory.

Songster

Al Ziryab, which means 'the blackbird', was a famous singer and musician in the 800s. He was born in Baghdad but was probably of African descent. At the Spanish Islamic court, Al Ziryab added a fifth string to the oud. He also used a vulture's quill on the strings instead of a wooden plectrum, to change its sound.

27

Around the world

c. 3000–1460 BCE Indus Valley
We know that Indus Valley peoples love dancing through dance poses sculpted in stone, bronze and terracotta. Stringed instruments, some like harps, are played.

900 CE Kingdom of Benin
Guilds of musicians play stringed instruments, hand clappers, bells, drums, flutes and horns. Court musicians accompany historians as they narrate deeds of past kings.

c. 900 CE Central America
Mayan musical instruments include flutes, panpipes, whistles and ocarinas that are shaped like animals. There are rattles, and drums made of wood or pottery.

DEATH AND DECLINE

Muslim burials are based on simplicity and purity. But there are grand Islamic mausoleums such as this 10th-century example from Bukhara city, in modern-day Uzbekistan. Inside lies the tomb of Ismail Samani, the founder of the Samanid dynasty at the end of the 800s. Bukhara was one of the cities that began to rival Baghdad.

28

Death of an empire

During the 900s, Abbasid rule over the Islamic world started to fracture, and Baghdad lost some of its power. African and Turkish slaves and slave soldiers, called Mamluks, started to rebel. North African territories pulled away from the Abbasids. However, in Spain, the grand Umayyad court at Cordoba continued to flourish. Baghdad's position at the heart of Islam turned to dust when the Mongols from Asia overthrew the Abbasids in 1258.

Ismail Samani's tomb, shown here, is made from highly patterned brickwork. The walls are so strong that they have never needed repair.

A place in heaven

To reach paradise, it is not enough for a Muslim to be buried according to Islamic customs. Muslims have to do good in this life. In the early Islamic golden age, caliphs and governors made sure that there were hospitals, lodgings for weary travellers and help for the poor. In Baghdad, skilled workers' guilds also provided shelter for travellers, care for orphans, and money to set up schools.

Beautiful tombs

Baghdad's ancient mausoleums have long gone. But we can get an idea of Abbasid tomb architecture in cities such as Bukhara. Many tombs are brick built and feature a dome. Elaborate, patterned brickwork and finely pierced stone windows show the skill and money lavished on those buried inside.

The Great Mosque of Samarra, in modern-day Iraq was built by the Abbasid Caliph, Al-Mutawakkil in the mid 9th century. Samarra became a temporary capital for the Abbasid caliphs.

 ## Around the world

c. 4000–2000 BCE Sumer
Ancient Sumerians are buried in the ground to be closer to other human souls. Sumer declines in 750 BCE when the city walls of Ur are battered by Amorites.

c. 900 CE Central America
Mayans are buried with maize in their mouths to symbolise their souls' rebirth. Bodies are sprinkled in red mineral dust, the colour of death, then wrapped in cotton.

900 CE Kingdom of Benin
Benin kings are buried in their ancient spiritual homeland city of Ile Ife to the north west. Benin declined in the 16th century and was ransacked by British forces in 1897.

GLOSSARY

Ambassador A ruler's representative in another country.

Artisan Skilled, expert craftsman or craftswoman.

Astrolabe Instrument for measuring the position of the stars, planets, Sun and Moon to calculate time and distance on Earth.

Astrology Study of the galaxies, Sun and Moon to predict the future.

Astronomy Study of the planets, stars, galaxies, Sun and Moon.

Barter Exchange goods rather than pay for them with money.

Caliph Islamic religious leader and political ruler.

Caravan A company of merchants or pilgrims travelling together with their animals.

Crucible Earthen pot used as a very hot oven, or kiln.

Dhow Sailing boat with triangular sails used by Arab traders to transport heavy goods.

Dinar Unit of money used across Islamic lands.

Hadith Collection of the deeds, sayings and teachings of the Prophet Muhammad (pbuh).

Jawla Grand Tour taken by rich Islamic tourists across many lands.

Kufic First Arabic script with many styles.

Oasis Natural patch of wetland in the middle of desert.

Oud Muslim lute.

Qibla Direction in which Muslims must face to pray, often indicated in a mosque by a niche called a mihrab.

Quadrant Instrument that helps calculate distances by measuring angles up to 90 degrees.

Rihla Muslim travel writer.

Sasanian Referring to an empire and people that existed in the area of modern-day Iran before the arrival of Islam.

Silk Road Ancient trade and cultural links from China to the Mediterranean.

Sorghum Grass types that provide cereal.

Steel Very hard metal made from iron ore and carbon used for sword blades and many other objects because of its strength.

Trigonometry Mathematics that measures the relationship of lengths and angles in triangles to calculate distance.

Wazir Islamic Minister, or advisor to a ruler.

Zij Numerical table used in astronomy to calculate the positions of the planets, stars, Sun and Moon.

WEBSITES

You can learn basic facts about Islam on:
http://www.bbc.co.uk/religion/religions/islam/ataglance/glance.shtml

Find out more about Islamic art on:
http://www.bbc.co.uk/religion/religions/islam/art/art_1.shtml

Take a look at Islamic architecture on:
http://www.bbc.co.uk/religion/religions/islam/art/architecture.shtml

You can find out about Islamic Spain, which developed at the same time as the Abbasid empire on:
http://www.bbc.co.uk/religion/religions/islam/history/spain_1.shtml

Note to parents and teachers
Every effort has been made by the Publishers to ensure that the websites in this book are suitable for children, that they are of the highest educational value, and that they contain no inappropriate or offensive material. However, because of the nature of the Internet, it is impossible to guarantee that the contents of these sites will not be altered. We strongly advise that Internet access is supervised by a responsible adult.

TIMELINE

632 The Holy Prophet Muhammad (pbuh) dies in Madinah, a desert city in Saudi Arabia. The first wars are waged by his father-in-law, Caliph Abu-Bakr.

711 Muslim soldiers conquer the Iberian peninsula — that's Portugal and Spain. They oust the ruling Visigoths from Cordoba.

752 Abbasid caliphs take over the Umayyads from their rule over Middle Eastern Islamic lands. Caliph al-Mansur makes Baghdad the region's capital.

756 Umayyad ruler, Abdul Rahman, creates an Umayyad Islamic state in Spain to rival the Abbasids in the Middle East.

762 Caliph al-Mansur begins to build the Abbasid capital in Baghdad.

767 An Islamic state is set up by Ibn Madrar at Sijilmasa in Africa.

786 Harun al-Rashid (reigned 786-809) becomes the Abbasid Caliph in Baghdad. He starts to build the House of Wisdom.

800 Algebra is invented by al-Khwarizmi, and science develops.

813 Al'Ma'mun (reigned 813-833), al-Rashid's son, finishes building the House of Wisdom. He gathers scientists and scholars, including Persians, Jews and Christians.

836 Abbasid caliphs move temporarily from Baghdad to a new capital, Samarra.

861 Turkish soldiers murder Caliph al-Mutawakkil, the ruler of Samarra, and disrupt the region until 945.

908 A weak Baghdadi ruler, al-Muqtadir, spends too much money and leads to the city's inevitable decline.

1258 Hulagu Khan and his Mongolian warriors sack Baghdad and destroy the House of Wisdom.

INDEX